ANOTHER TREE
in the yard

written by Lucia Sera
illustrated by John Iorio

VOCALIS LTD
-Waterbury-

Vocalis Fiction, a division of Vocalis Ltd.
100 Avalon Circle, Waterbury, Connecticut 06710, U.S.A.

The text of this book is set in 14 pt. Times. The illustrations are in watercolor. Printed and bound in the U.S.A.

Library of Congress Cataloging-in-Publication Data

Sera, Lucia Sera, 1963-
Another Tree in the yard / written by Lucia Sera ; illustrated by John Iorio.
    p. cm.
 Summary: Maggie, a magnolia tree, was planted for luck when the Soto family moved into their first house, so when they decide to add a second tree--just when they are adding a second child--she is jealous and resentful.
 ISBN 1-932653-36-8 (alk. paper)
[1. Jealousy--Fiction. 2. Sibling rivalry--Fiction. 3. Magnolias--Fiction. 4. Figs--Fiction. 5. Trees--Fiction.] I. Iorio, John, ill. II Title.
  PZ7.S4798An2004
  [E]--dc22
                                                  2004041919

        10 09 08 07 06 05 04   10 9 8 7 6 5 4 3 2 1

                        FIRST IMPRESSION

for Emily and Erin

When the Soto family moved into their first hou

y planted a tree in the yard for good luck.

Some years went by . . .

and the tree flourished,

growing into a *magnificent magnol*

e Soto's little girl, Julia, called her "Maggie."

Not only was Maggie beautiful, but she blended right in with the family's life.

Shade from her blossoms kept the house cool in the sun.

One of her long branches held an end of the clothesline.

Her full foliage made for a well-padded hangout.

Her flowers were gathered for indoor enjoyment.

And her fallen twigs crackled in cozy fires.

No one could deny what a great tree Maggie was.

Indeed, people who stopped by would remark of her rosy bloom:

"Why, it's the very picture of health!"

and

"Now that's a tree to be reckoned with!"

and

"It looks like a pink cloud." (A child pointed out.)

As it happened, the Sotos enjoyed having the tree so much that .   .   .

. . . they decided to get another tree.

Which kind would it be? What would it look like? There was much discussion in the household, and finally they chose a fig tree. "It'll make a nice friend for our first one," the Soto parents agreed. "Just like the new baby coming will be a companion for you, Julia." They had found out ahead of time that it was going to be a boy.

The magnolia heard them talking . . .

and, truth be told, had mixed feelings,

such as:

"Nobody asked me if *I* wanted another tree," and worse,
"Things are fine as they are. I don't *want* any changes."

——— but on the other hand, she reasoned ———

"Well, it might be interesting– only for a while, though."

On the day the new tree arrived from the nursery, there was a buzz of activity.

First, a truck came carrying in the special delivery.

Next, a good location was loudly debated and decided.

And then, a bed was prepared to plant him in.

Maggie tried to be as positive as possible. "Patience is the name of the game," she kept telling herself. Just the same, the fuss *was* a bit irritating. What was the big deal over a silly sapling, anyway? Oh, in their haste, the helpers trampled over her outer roots. That was not fun. In fact, the whole day was filled with upset. Maggie felt forgotten about in all the hubbub.

Things improved somewhat when Julia threw her arms around Maggie and promised, "But I'll always love *you*!" It was like balm on her weary bark. "Huh!" thought Maggie, "at least *someone* around here appreciates me."

So, the little tree settled in. Everyone's attention turned to this baby fig– even the neighbors oohed and aahed. Brother! It was obvious to Maggie that they couldn't hear what a racket he made with his bare branches flailing back and forth, especially at nighttime. (Meanwhile, there was a baby boy *inside* the house kicking up a storm; a frolicking Félix had just joined the Soto family.)

Another annoyance was that this newcomer drank up a lot of the water in the ground. It's true that there was plenty to go around, but *still* . . . "When you're used to having something all to yourself, nobody should be allowed to touch it without your permission," Maggie secretly grumbled, as she looked on at the unwelcome guest.

Maggie stared in silence. "Just LOOK at him, spreading his roots like he owns the place. When's he going back to where he came from, I wonder. Things were better before. . . . "

The new fig tree, named "Figaro" by the family, was certainly making himself at home.

After a few months, the air had taken on a distinct chill. . . .
Maggie noticed Figaro shivering against the wind that winter.
One particularly cold night, he turned pale with frost.

Maggie found herself bowing over to protect him from the elements. When she
looked down, she could see that the spindly tree had become wet– for all of the tiny
icicles had melted in the warmth of Maggie's arms and were dripping tears of relief.

"It was nothing," dismissed the older tree. "I couldn't let him just freeze like that."
However, it was her own coldness toward Figaro that had begun to thaw out.
She sighed, "I suppose he's here to stay, so I might as well make the best of it."

In the spring, some of the birds which usually sat in Maggie's branches took their perch over to Figaro's. His rugged bark presented a curious challenge.

Fanning her petals in the breeze, Maggie declared, "Fine by me. I'd been planning to cut back on my flock parties *anyway* – always such a mess to clean up after."

Summer soon came with its scorcher days. Maggie would let Figaro tuck himself under her branches in the afternoons when the sun was strongest. "Of course, I am taller and more mature," she proudly noted to herself. "Without my shading, that twig would probably end up withering away."

From her window, Julia had watched the young tree bud and become thick with leaves. It was like little Félix's hair, growing bushier by the day. Maybe he *was* as cute as everyone said. "When he gets older, I'll show him how to climb up a tree trunk. He can have the fig, and I'll stick with the magnolia," Julia planned.

One season turned into the next, and somehow Maggie got used to Figaro being there. *Actually . . .* she was amused at all his doings:

he grew knotted with muscles
(and constantly flexed them),

faded yellow in the fall,

went bald in the winter

and sprouted figs in the spring.

The changes were interesting.

And Maggie had to admit,

he
made
the rainy
days a little
less lonely.

Figaro, in turn, became so fond of Maggie that one day he reached out and said, "I love you."

The two trees liked to form a tent by joining their branches together and letting them hang down to the ground. Their canopy of thick, green leaves created the effect of being deep in a lush forest. Naturally, the children were drawn to this enchanting hide-out. They were there all the time, never noticing the hours gone by absorbed in play.

Once, when a huge, unknown dog came dancing down the street, Julia and Félix ran as fast as they could and hid in the tree-fort.

Occasionally, they brought their sleeping bags out and stayed the night under the trees (whose gentle swaying lulled them to sleep).

Often, Mrs. Soto would read stories there to the delight of all the neighborhood kids, who let their imaginations carry them away.

Maggie and Figaro were happy to have so much laughter around them.

Time tumbled forward, and Figaro turned out to be a big-hearted, healthy fellow. He had long been shouldering his share of the harsh weather, often shielding Maggie. She remembered with regret how put out she had felt at first. They had gone through a lot over the years together, always standing side by side.

Maggie now saw that Figaro had made all of the good times better– how entertaining he could be with his many jokes, stunts and random acts of *silliness*!

An example was the clever contortion trick he did with his trunk.

(But when he would go into tickle mode
~ just watch out ~
sometimes it was *too much* nonsense,
and Maggie would have to draw the line.)

Along the way, they had become the best of friends. And Maggie couldn't imagine how life would have been *without* this funny tree she had come to love.

In time, they both realized that the children (who by now had grown up) were r
interested in playing in their branches anymore . . . but they would always ha
each other to keep company.

Maggie concluded, "It turns out, after all is said and do

a WONDERFUL thing to have a brother tree in the yard."

The end.